Beside the Seaside

Daniel Hanton

For Grace and Elsie

This book belongs to

. . . .

GE
BOOKS

Splash went the milk in the breakfast bowl,
then off to the beach for a morning stroll.

Ding! The bus bell rang at the stop,
the bus doors open and off they hop.

Sqwark said the seagulls as they watched family day trips,
perhaps today they might have chips.

Splosh went the feet paddling in the sea,
while Pops watched on, sipping his tea.

Click! The case was opened by the man in the smart straw hat,
he began to build a tent on a bright coloured mat.

Giggles of excitement were heard across the skies,
a colourful little puppet theatre grew before your eyes.

Hee-haw said the donkey plodding past the show,
she popped her head around the back and did not want to go.

Clang went the bell, you could hear it down the prom.
Everyone came to see where the noise was coming from.

Tiddley-om-pom-pom! The music began to play,
oh we do like to be beside the seaside a funny voice did say.

Swoosh went the curtains with a great big cheer,
the children waiting patiently for someone to appear.

Whizz! As if by magic appears the clown called Joey.
He's from London and his clothes are bright and showy.

Root, toot, toot! Mister Punch arrives with his big hooked nose.
Full of laughter wearing red and yellow clothes.

Kissy, kissy, kissy! Mister Punch's wife Judy gives him a great big kiss,
he looks after the baby which he thinks is bliss.

Whaaa! The baby's dressed in pink all spotty,
he cries for his mummy and needs the potty.

Sizzle! Joey has cooked sausages in time for tea,
Mister Punch is happy and full of glee.

Snap! Mister Punch did not see the hungry crocodile,
all big and green with a great big smile.

Chomp! He eats the sausages with one big bite.
The greedy, green crocodile was not polite.

Boo! Mister Punch is scared by a floating ghost,
Punch gets the ghost and the ghost is toast.

Hooray! It is time to go back down below,
until another day we can say hello.

Jingle went the coins as they dropped into the bag,
to thank the Punch and Judy man, a lovely time we had.

Clatter is the sound of packing all away,
it is home time now but we have had a lovely day.

Many thanks to my family and Punch and Judy friends for their help and support.

G&E Books

First published in Great Britain 2021

Text copyright © Daniel Hanton 2021
Illustrations copyright © Daniel Hanton 2021

ISBN 978-1-5272-8670-2

Printed in Great Britain

GE
BOOKS